This Walker book belongs to:

_____

_____

_____

For Grace Holly   C.M.

First published 2011 by Walker Books Ltd

87 Vauxhall Walk, London SE11 5HJ

This edition published 2012

2 4 6 8 10 9 7 5 3 1

Text © 2011 Colin McNaughton

Illustrations © 2011 Emma Chichester Clark

The right of Colin McNaughton and Emma Chichester Clark to be identified
as author and illustrator respectively of this work has been asserted by them
in accordance with the Copyright, Designs and Patents Act 1988

This book has been typeset in Horley Old Style MT

Printed in China

British Library Cataloguing in Publication Data:
a catalogue record for this book is available from the British Library

ISBN 978-1-4063-3835-5

www.walker.co.uk

WALKER BOOKS
AND SUBSIDIARIES
LONDON • BOSTON • SYDNEY • AUCKLAND

Have You Ever Ever Ever?

Colin McNaughton

Illustrated by Emma Chichester Clark

Have you ever, ever, ever
In your incy-wincy life
Seen an incy-wincy spider
With his incy-wincy wife?

No, I've never, never, never
In my incy-wincy life
Seen an incy-wincy spider
With his incy-wincy wife.

Have you ever, ever, ever
In your diddle-diddle life
Seen a cat and a fiddle
With his diddle-diddle wife?

No, I've never, never, never
In my diddle-diddle life
Seen a cat and a fiddle
With his diddle-diddle wife.

Have you ever, ever, ever
In your goosey gander life
Seen a goosey gander wander
With his goosey gander wife?

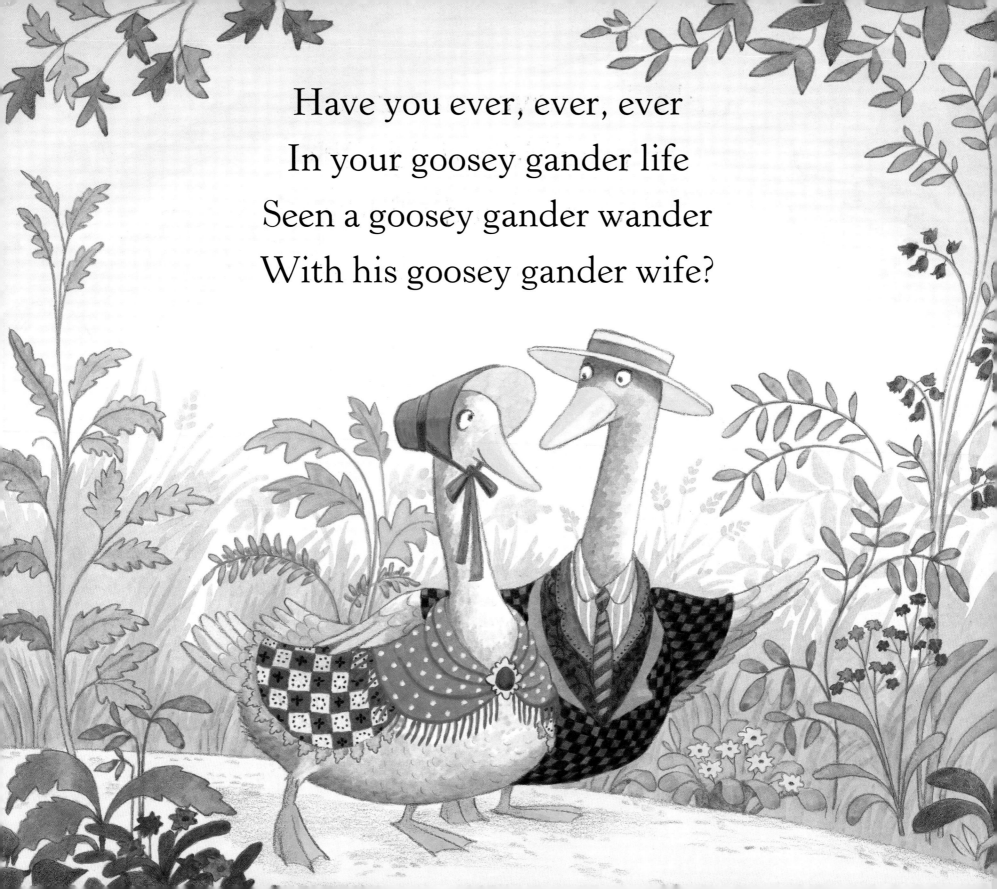

No, I've never, never, never
In my goosey gander life
Seen a goosey gander wander
With his goosey gander wife.

Have you ever, ever, ever
In your Bonny Bobby life
Seen a Bonny Bobby Shaftoe
With his Bonny Bobby wife?

No, I've never, never, never
In my Bonny Bobby life
Seen a Bonny Bobby Shaftoe
With his Bonny Bobby wife.

Have you ever, ever, ever
In your Punchinello life
Seen a Punchinello bellow
At his Punchinello wife?

No, I've never, never, never
In my Punchinello life
Seen a Punchinello bellow
At his Punchinello wife.

Have you ever, ever, ever
In your four and twenty lives
Seen four and twenty blackbirds
With their four and twenty wives?

No, I've never, never, never
In my four and twenty lives
Seen four and twenty blackbirds
With their four and twenty wives.

Have you ever, ever, ever
In your cock-a-doodle life
Seen a cock-a-doodle doodle
With his cock-a-doodle wife?

No, I've never, never, never
In my pickled pepper life
Seen a Peter Piper pick
A pickled pepper for his wife.

Have you ever, ever, ever
In your doodle-dandy life
Seen a Yankee doodle dandy
With his Yankee doodle wife?

No, I've never, never, never
In my doodle-dandy life
Seen a Yankee doodle dandy
With his Yankee doodle wife.

Well I never, never, never!
They live right behind this door.
I've told you of a few
But there are many, many more…

Let me introduce –
the friends of **Mother Goose!**

Also by Colin McNaughton and Emma Chichester Clark

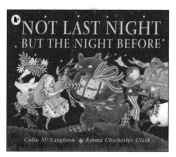

978-1-4063-2556-0

Other books by Colin McNaughton

  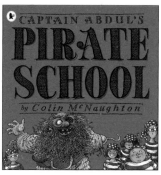  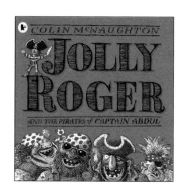

978-1-4063-1352-9   978-0-7445-4394-0   978-0-7445-9896-4   978-1-4063-0585-2   978-1-84428-478-8

Other books by Emma Chichester Clark

 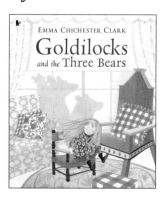 

978-1-4063-2620-8   978-1-4063-3075-5   978-1-4063-1511-0

Available from all good booksellers

www.walker.co.uk